The Usborne Official

Princess Handbook

HRH Princess Rosalinda
(with help from her most trusted lady-in-waiting
Susanna Davidson)

Illustrations inked with most exceptional skill by
Lord Mike and Lord Carl Gordon

Designed according to elegant arrangements by
Lady Joanne Kirkby, Earl Marc Maynard
and Duchess Nayera Everall

Contents

Dear princess-in-the-making,

Welcome to my TOP SECRET
guide to becoming a true princess.

As my fairy godmother says, every girl
has an inner princess – you just need
to find her. Study my handbook and
I'll teach you everything you need to
know to become a perfect princess.

Good luck!

Yours most royally,
Princess Rosalinda

Chapter 1
How to be a princess

Princesses have wonderful lives. They live in palaces, dance at balls and dine with princes. But there's more to being a princess than traipsing around in tiaras. You also need to know how to behave like one...

Handsome prince visiting me

My bedroom

My pet cat, Emperpuss

Me, outside my palace home

The first step to becoming a princess is to be helpful...

and polite.

Thank you.
Odd socks are just what I wanted for my birthday.

A true princess is
kind to everyone...

and wouldn't
dream of losing
her temper.

A princess NEVER goes off in a huff...

...or makes a fuss.

Yes, you've got it. Being a princess is HARD.

Princess role models

To become a true princess, you need a ROLE MODEL. Then, the next time you want to scream and shout, take a deep breath. Think how your ROLE MODEL would behave, and try to be like her. Here are some suggestions, taken from my top four fairy tales...

Cinderella

Popularity	99
Brains	60
Beauty	90

Good, kind and obedient, Cinderella worked for her horrible stepsisters for years without complaining. Think patience and virtue.

Snow White

Popularity	88
Brains	40
Beauty	100

Snow White was kind and beautiful. She loved housework, singing and dancing in woods. A stay-at-home style princess.

Ariel

Popularity	75
Brains	92
Beauty	93

Okay, so she's a mermaid, but in spite of her tail she still makes a great role model: bold, brave and free-spirited.

Sleeping Beauty

Popularity	78
Brains	99
Beauty	99

Beautiful, graceful, clever, musical... you name the quality, SB had it. If you want to be a perfect princess, aim to be like Sleeping Beauty.

Or, of course, you could choose *me* as your ROLE MODEL...

Princess Rosalinda

Naughtiness	99
Fun	99
Sense of adventure	99

I'm not totally perfect. No housework or hundred years of sleep for me. But like all true princesses, I do try to be helpful, polite and kind.

In case you were wondering, here are some role models you shouldn't choose...

The Snow Queen

Popularity	2
Brains	90
Beauty	92

Frosty, cruel and power crazy, the Snow Queen gives off extremely bad vibes. She's beautiful and brainy, but avoid if you want to keep your friends.

Cinderella's ugly stepsister

Popularity	1
Brains	12
Beauty	0

Cinderella's stepsister is mean, moody and miserable. She may have good connections, but she's got none of the qualities of a true princess.

Perhaps you have your own role models in mind? Fill in the role model cards below...

Fairy tales aren't just good for role models. They are full of tips on how to become a true princess. If you haven't read them for a while, you may want to follow our fairy tale lesson plan below...

Useful fairy tale lesson 1

Marry a prince

If it worked for Cinderella, it could work for you. By marrying Prince Charming, she went from servant girl to princess in one easy step.
But where do you find your prince?

Places for picking up princes...

1. AT A ROYAL BALL

All you need is a ballgown and glass slippers. (Cinderella wore a pair and Prince Charming fell instantly in love.)

2. INSIDE A HAIRY BEAST OR A BEAR

Yes, really. Beasts and bears can be handsome princes under evil spells (you can tell by the fact that they talk). To break the spell, you have to prove that you truly, truly love your beast/bear. This can take years.

3. AT A BANQUET

Princes tend to be a hungry bunch – it's all the energy they waste chasing dragons. That's why banquets are great places for meeting them (if you can tear them away from the food, that is).

4. UP A TOWER

Find a room at the very top and... wait. But be warned – it could take years. Rapunzel waited so long her hair grew as long as a ladder (rather handily, as it turned out).

5. INSIDE A FROG

Evil witches also love turning princes into these webbed wonders. But how do you tell if there's a prince under all that green? Find out on page 20.

6. NEAR A DRAGON

Princes love saving princesses from the clutches of these beasts. Just make sure you don't get toasted first.

I know, I know... Finding a prince is complicated!
Try this quiz to help you on your way.

Who is your perfect prince?

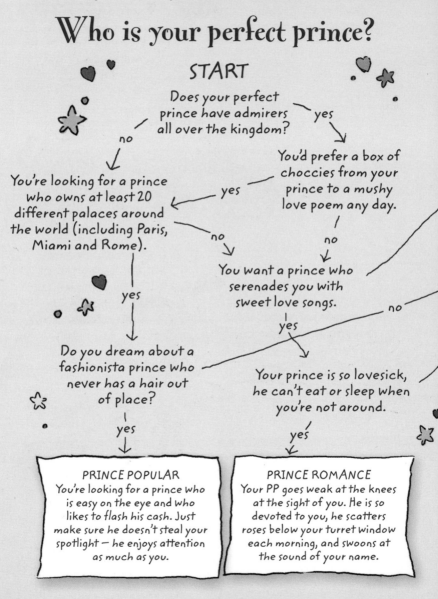

START

Does your perfect prince have admirers all over the kingdom?

yes

no

You'd prefer a box of choccies from your prince to a mushy love poem any day.

You're looking for a prince who owns at least 20 different palaces around the world (including Paris, Miami and Rome).

yes

no

no

You want a prince who serenades you with sweet love songs.

yes

Do you dream about a fashionista prince who never has a hair out of place?

no

yes

yes

Your prince is so lovesick, he can't eat or sleep when you're not around.

yes

PRINCE POPULAR
You're looking for a prince who is easy on the eye and who likes to flash his cash. Just make sure he doesn't steal your spotlight — he enjoys attention as much as you.

PRINCE ROMANCE
Your PP goes weak at the knees at the sight of you. He is so devoted to you, he scatters roses below your turret window each morning, and swoons at the sound of your name.

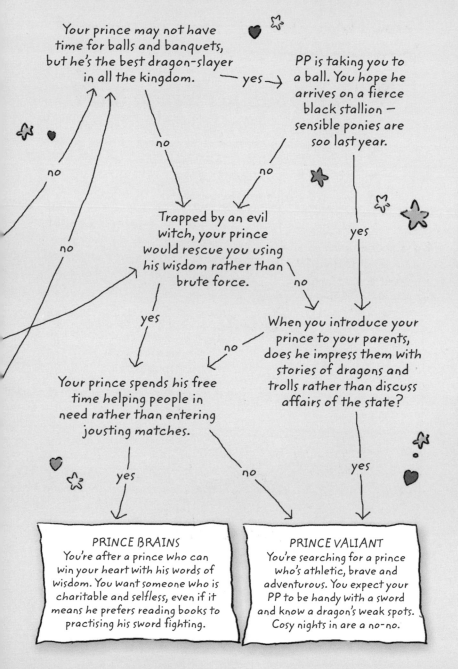

Your prince may not have time for balls and banquets, but he's the best dragon-slayer in all the kingdom. — yes →

PP is taking you to a ball. You hope he arrives on a fierce black stallion — sensible ponies are soo last year.

no

no

no

no

yes

Trapped by an evil witch, your prince would rescue you using his wisdom rather than brute force.

no

yes

When you introduce your prince to your parents, does he impress them with stories of dragons and trolls rather than discuss affairs of the state?

no

Your prince spends his free time helping people in need rather than entering jousting matches.

yes

no

yes

PRINCE BRAINS
You're after a prince who can win your heart with his words of wisdom. You want someone who is charitable and selfless, even if it means he prefers reading books to practising his sword fighting.

PRINCE VALIANT
You're searching for a prince who's athletic, brave and adventurous. You expect your PP to be handy with a sword and know a dragon's weak spots. Cosy nights in are a no-no.

Is he a frog, or a prince?

Find out with our quick guide

1. First, you need to know your frogs from your toads.

Slimy skin

Frog
(but possibly a prince)

Warty

Dry skin

Toad
(just a toad)

2. Then you need to kiss him! This is the **only** way to break the spell. Not all frogs are princes, so you may have to kiss a lot of frogs before you find your prince...

Useful fairy tale lesson 2

Pass the Pea Test

According to *The Princess and the Pea*, the test to see if you're a true princess is if you're sensitive enough to feel a pea under twenty mattresses.

It's that simple – find your pea and you've proved you're a princess. Unfortunately, the Pea Test is rather tricky to pass.

Princes' mothers have been
known to use old, mushy peas,
that are very hard to feel.

Ye Royal
Pea

So how can you make
sure you succeed?

Is there a pea in my bed?

Find out with our quick guide

1. You won't be able to feel that pea unless you're prepared. Put a pea under one mattress, see if you can feel it, then gradually work your way up to twenty.

2. Get ready to cheat. If you're ever put in a bed with more than one mattress and a prince asks how you slept, simply say:

Very badly, there was a pea in my bed.

In that case, you must be a true princess.

Useful fairy tale lesson 3

Find a fairy godmother

Your life as a princess will be a lot easier if you have a fairy godmother. If yours is anything like Cinderella's, she'll give you advice, guide you through danger...

...and most important of all, magic you up a dress for your first princess ball.

But if you don't have one, don't worry! To make sure you don't miss out, I've asked my fairy godmother to pass on some advice...

Remember, nothing is what it seems!

1. EVIL QUEENS

Snow White had one for a stepmother, who tried to kill her FOUR times. Not to be trusted.

2. SPINNING WHEEL

Sleeping Beauty pricked her finger on one of these, and it sent her to sleep for a hundred years. Don't touch them.

3. TROLLS

Often employed by evil queens to do away with princesses. Luckily, they are very stupid and easy to outwit.

4. NASTY FAIRIES

Just because she has wings and a wand, doesn't mean she's good. A fairy cursed Sleeping Beauty, while another one put a spell on Beauty's Beast.

5. POISONOUS OBJECTS

Treat all gifts with suspicion. Snow White's stepmother used poisoned lace, then a comb and finally an apple to try to kill Snow White.

So, do you think you've got what it takes to be a princess? Find out with my Princess Test...

The Princess Test

1. Your evil stepmother is making you cook and clean for your ugly stepsisters. Do you:

My stepmother

(a) Do what your stepmother says, but complain *all* the time?

(b) Work as hard as you can, but sneak out whenever there's a royal ball?

(c) Refuse to do it – after all, no princess ever worked as a servant?

2. You are staying in a castle where you've been given a bed piled high with mattresses. Do you:

(a) Use the bed as a trampoline?

(b) Quickly hunt around for peas?

(c) Order the servants to remove the mattresses, as they are rather hard to climb?

3. Kidnapped at birth by a wicked witch, you have always dreamed of being rescued by a handsome prince. In the meantime, do you:

(a) Take up sewing?

(b) Grow your hair?

(c) Shout for help?

4. Your golden ball has been rescued from a palace pond by a wet and slimy frog. In return, he asks to share your palace home. Do you:

(a) Just say "no!" Princesses should have nothing to do with frogs?

(b) Say "no!" but then kiss him anyway?

(c) Fry him in butter?

5. A handsome prince is hosting a ball and you are invited. Shopping for an outfit, you spot some glass slippers.
Do you:

(a) Try them on, but decide against them because glass pinches your toes?

(b) Buy them immediately – glass slippers are the perfect accessory for any dress?

(c) Ask the shop assistant if they are dishwasher safe?

If you answered...

Mostly As:

You're on the right track: you just need to brush up on your fairytales.

Mostly Bs:

Congratulations! You are clearly a princess at heart.

Mostly Cs:

You haven't been paying attention. Go back to the beginning of this book and start again.

Chapter 2
Live like a princess

A princess needs to know her way around her palace homes. After all, you don't want to miss out on glamorous balls just because you wandered into the wrong wing.

Naturally, you'll have more than one home. There'll be the royal residence in town...

...the palace in the country...

...the winter castle in the mountains...

...and the summer palace by the sea.

My glam older sister at our summer pad

Upon entering each home, your priorities are as follows:

1) Discover the back stairs to the chef's kitchen, so you can sneak down for midnight treats.

2) Test the ballroom floors to see if they make good skidding surfaces.

3) Find the best bannisters for sliding down.

4) Locate HIDING PLACES, so you can escape from visiting duchesses with bristly chins.

Me, escaping from Great-Aunt Esmerelda

Hiding place

Introducing your servants

You'll have lots of servants to help you find your way around. Here's a guide of everyone who works for you. Prepare to meet your...

Ladies-in-waiting

Job: *star servants & best friends*

What they do: *come with you on trips abroad, help you out at grand occasions and out of any tricky situations...*

Equerry

Job: *a male lady-in-waiting*

What he does: *he has a funny name but an important job. With his army training, he is there to save you from danger.*

Butler

Job: to serve your every need

What he does: dusts the furniture, pours your drinks, serves your food and keeps your secrets.

Laundry maid

Job: makes your clothes look spotless

What she does: Washes and irons everything in your wardrobe, including your underwear.

Private secretary

Job: *your walking, talking diary*

What he does: *deals with the press, keeps you up to date on important matters and, best of all, arranges fabulous photoshoots.*

Personal photographer

Job: *your most trusted photographer*

What he does: *Always makes you look as glam as possible – soft lighting is the key.*

Dresser

Job: *to make you look wonderful*

What she does: *comes with you on shopping trips and tells you what's hot and what's not.*

Dressmaker

Job: *designs couture dresses for any occassion*

What she does: *creates fabulous gowns so you never have to wear the same thing twice.*

Coachman

Job: transports you to and from every engagement

What he does: Available at any hour of the day, he carries you and your entourage wherever you need to go.

I always travel light.

Letter writer

Job: *to sort through your never-ending fan mail*

What she does: *counts your hundreds of letters each day and even replies to them for you.*

There are also hundreds of other people at work behind the scenes.

1. Chefs

The top cooks in the country, who will prepare mouthwatering meals of your choice for you and your guests.

2. Footmen

Help serve your meals, light your fires, look after your pets and ride behind carriages at grand events.

3. Pages

Supervise the arrival
and departure of
your fans (and other
visitors), help serve
your meals and best of
all, tidy up after you.

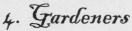

4. Gardeners

Ferociously tend
and guard the
fabulous flowers in
the palace gardens.

5. Housemaids

Dust, clean and attend to your every need. You need never make your bed again.

6. The palace ghosts

Great at scaring away unwanted visitors (once you've got used to them, that is).

How to deal with servants

It's very important to treat your servants properly. You'll need to learn their names, be polite and never, ever snap at them. You should also listen to what your servants have to tell you.

BLEURGH!

In China it's polite to belch during meals... but NOWHERE else.

Private secretary

Any servant who is rude, or is known to tell palace secrets, should be fired – immediately. But those who are loyal and supportive should be rewarded with kindliness and smiles.

How your servants should treat you

1. Your servants should address you as **Your Royal Highness** at all times. Nicknames (pet, dearie, princess etc.) are not permitted.

2. Naturally, your servants will bow or curtsey to you. The rule is twice a day – once in the morning and once in the afternoon. **Expect no less.**

3. It goes without saying that servants should **never** disagree with you. You are always right. Enough said.

4. Servants are required to provide foot rubs **at your request**. Those who refuse or show any signs of disgust will not be tolerated.

Once you are queen, though, it gets even
better. Then servants are expected
to walk out backwards,
bowing as they go...

A pleasure to be of
service, Your Majesty.

Secret signals

Your servants are also your link to the outside world. They'll fill you in on the latest gossip and come to your aid when you're out and about. For the best results, work on some secret signals with your ladies-in-waiting first.

1. SNEEZING
You've got toilet paper stuck to your shoe.

2. PATTING HAIR
Don't kiss Prince Ferdinand.
He has sweaty cheeks.

3. HAND ON CHEEK
Be kind to Prince Nigel.
He's in love with you.

4. HANDS ON HIPS

Hide! Your Great-Aunt Esmerelda (with the bristly chin) is looking for you.

5. WINKING

Don't go too near Prince Stinkerdink. He smells cabbagey.

But no matter how close you are to your servants, NEVER gossip with them. It's very un-princess-y. If you are bursting to tell a secret, try writing it down in your Top Secret Royal Diary.

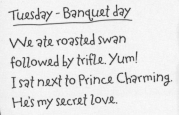

Tuesday - Banquet day

We ate roasted swan followed by trifle. Yum! I sat next to Prince Charming. He's my secret love.

Wednesday - Royal ball

The king split his trousers dancing the polka. He quickly covered his bottom with a napkin but guess what I saw... leopard-skin bloomers! Shhh!

I ♥ P.C.

Use this space to write your own Royal Secrets: (I won't read them, I promise...)

My name is Princess ....

....

I live in... (Describe your castle or home)

....

....

....

My hobbies include ....

....

....

....

....

....

My secret crush is ....

....

....

He lives in... (A castle in the mountains? A palace
in the Bahamas?)

....

....

I met him at... (A banquet? Up a tower?)........................

....

....

His hobbies include.... (Jousting? Dragon spotting?)

....

....

....

My best lady-in-waiting is ....
....
....

I like her because... (Is she loyal? Kind?)
....
....

....

When I am queen, I will... (Ban homework?
Create three day weekends?)
....
....
....

....

Chapter 3
How to dress

As a princess, you are expected always to look your best. Your clothes are a chance to show off your sparkling personality, but they also need careful thought and attention...

After all, ma'am, you are representing your country.

Everyday wear

A hundred years ago, everyday wear for a princess meant a dress. And not just any dress — you'd be wearing lace petticoats, floaty fabrics, flowers, frills, ruffles and ribbons...

THE OLD DAYS

...but times have changed. These days, a princess can get away with jeans and flip-flops — as long as she stands out from the crowd.

Here are a few key fashion rules
to help you on your way...

Fashion do's...

As styled by my big sis,
Princess Ursulina

No princess should be
seen out and about
without her half-tiara.

Sunglasses are good
for looking cool.

Brush your hair
until it shines
(a tip from
Rapunzel).

Wear jewels
that sparkle.

Keep up-to-
date with the
latest look.

FASHION
NEWS

Stay crease-free by
making sure your maid
irons the clothes you
plan to wear.

Fashion don't's...

Remember to keep clean! You can only sparkle if you're spotless.

Don't cake yourself in make-up. It can be very unattractive.

Avoid clothes with logos splashed all over them. You're a princess – you don't need them!

Don't get caught out in the cold – always carry a wrap or cardigan with you.

Comfort is important, but not to the point of looking sloppy.

...but remember – you're a princess. You can make up rules of your own!

You'll need a different outfit for every kind of occasion. Here's my quick guide to what to wear when you're out and about.

1. WALKABOUTS

involve (you guessed it) lots of walking, so choose clothes that are pretty but comfortable, such as flowery skirts, floaty tops, cute necklaces, pixie boots or pumps.

I'm trying to walk in heels, Emperpuss. Don't laugh at me.

2. TEA PARTIES

are very similar to lunch parties, but even more fun as you get to wear pretty scarves, little hats and matching gloves.

Friday - tea party
Time to accessorize...

Pretty necklace

Hat

Gloves

DAILY NEWS

EXCLUSIVE

GLAM PRINCESS

3. MOVIE PREMIERES

are your chance to shine. Think long gloves, sparkly jewels and stunning dresses.

4. BALLS

are the most glam occasions of all. Start planning at least six months in advance and demand the very best — silk, satins, shiny shoes and diamond tiaras.

Now it's your turn to design your own outfits.
I've added some suggestions for inspiration.

Summer tea party

Flowery
dress

Fan

Straw
hat

Pumps

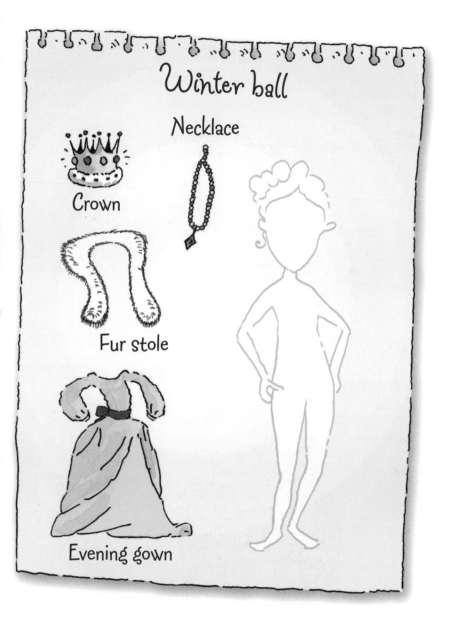

Winter ball

Crown

Necklace

Fur stole

Evening gown

Dressing for a ball

Here are five top tips to make sure you look your very best at your first royal ball:

Rule 1 Go long if you want to look glam (but don't choose a dress that's longer than you).

Rule 2 Wear flowers in your hair – they'll look lovely and smell gorgeous. You can hold them in with hair clips.

I'd advise roses,   daisies,   or freesias.

Always carry a wrap or a shawl to avoid goosebumps.

 Ask your dresser to add diamonds to your gown. A princess should sparkle as she moves.

 Don't forget to carry a fan – excellent for hiding behind or for attracting handsome princes.

Princess hairstyles

A princess should take good care of her hair.
Wash it often, brush it at least a hundred times
a day, and take out all hair accessories before you
go to sleep. This will keep it sleek and shiny.

You can also keep your fashion followers on their
toes by regularly changing your hairstyle. Your
stylist will have ideas of her own, but here are
a few suggestions. Try them out in front of the
mirror to see which suits you best.

French bun:
Be a beautiful ballerina
for a day

Rapunzel:
Keep your locks long
for visiting princes

Bunches:
Cute and casual,
but can't be worn
with a crown

Ringlets:
Very princessy,
so perfect for
state occasions

Big bow:
A real granny-pleaser –
try it at family parties

Pretty hairband:
Sweet & charming –
perfect for picnics

If you're a budding hair stylist yourself, you could experiment with your own styles here.

Accessorizing

A princess should always carry a handbag. Make sure it goes with your outfit and that it contains these important princess items:

1. Small mirror ☐

2. Gold-plated phone ☐

3. Silver comb ☐

4. Silk fan ☐

5. Sparkly purse ☐

6. Linen hanky ☐

Don't worry too much about the size of your bag. Heavy items can always be carried by one of your servants.

You've got your outfit and your accessories – now you just need to feel confident about what you're wearing. Before you leave the palace, spend time in front of your wall-to-wall mirrors so you can see yourself from all angles.

Finally, don't forget those small but important details...

☐ 1. Hair freshly combed
☐ 2. No creases in clothes
☐ 3. Skirt not tucked into underwear
☐ 4. Clean hanky

Rules about jewels

Even though you might want to pile on every jewel in your collection, you need to follow the Jewel Rules.

Rule 1

Young princesses are expected to wear corals and pearls. You will have to wait until you are older before you can wear diamonds and rubies.

Rule 2

Too many jewels at once are VULGAR. You can wear either large earrings or an extravagant necklace, but not both together.

The Christmas tree look should be avoided. →

Rule 3

Sadly, royal rules say that until your wedding day you can only wear half-tiaras, which are like silver hairbands with a jewel in the middle.

← These rules don't apply to pets, of course.

Once you are married, you can wear your tiara with pride. There are many different styles...

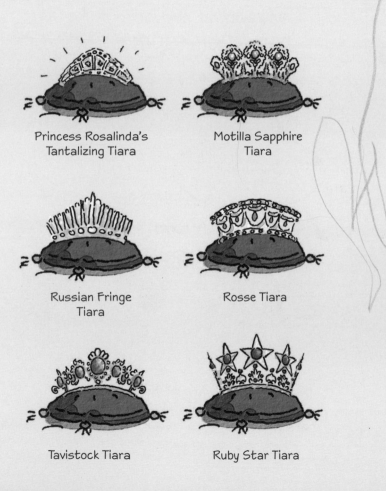

Princess Rosalinda's
Tantalizing Tiara

Motilla Sapphire
Tiara

Russian Fringe
Tiara

Rosse Tiara

Tavistock Tiara

Ruby Star Tiara

Just make sure that you wear your
tiaras with care...

A cautionary tale

Once upon a time, at a grand royal
event, two elderly duchesses were talking
together. As they bent nearer each other,
their tiaras became locked together, like
the antlers of fighting stags.

> Do you think we'll
> always be like this?

> This is
> tiarifying!

They were stuck like that for HOURS. A
goldsmith had to be called in to free them.

Chapter 4
How to move

As a true princess, you need to be graceful at all times, from the turn of your head to the sweep of your curtsey. That means no tripping, no falling, no slouching, no plodding...

So, do you walk like a peasant or a princess? Take this test to find out...

Are you gliding gracefully?

1. Try walking with your crown on your head (or a book, if you don't happen to have your crown handy).

   What happens?

   (a) It balances perfectly.

   (b) It falls off.

   (c) You're not even going to try. You'd rather spend your time watching the palace paint dry.

2. Walk past a mirror and look at your arms.

What are they doing?

(a) They're swinging by your sides in soft, ballet-like movements.

(b) Flapping like a turkey in trouble.

(c) Moving like a soldier's under marching orders.

3. Walk ten steps forwards.

Where are you now?

(a) Not much further from where you started. You only take very dainty steps.

(b) In pain, not having spotted the furniture in the way.

(c) Near to Planet Zog, on the outer rim of the galaxy. Your speedy strides mean you cover huge distances in no time.

4. How do you walk down the stairs?

(a) You skip gracefully.

(b) You generally trip, fall, then clutch the bannisters for dear life.

(c) You make the stairs shudder beneath your pounding feet.

If you answered:

Mostly As:

Congratulations!

You have the grace of a swan and are already gliding like a princess.

Mostly Bs:

You are a clumsy duckling. But don't fret. There is still time to improve. Just take small, dainty steps.

Mostly Cs:

Go back to page 5 of this book and start again.

You are clearly missing the point of what it means to be a princess.

Running

There is not a huge amount to say about princesses and running, as the rule is quite simple: princesses don't run. Ever?............ No! Not even if they are being chased by a giant hairy spider or a fire-breathing dragon.

Aren't you going to run?

No! I'm a princess.

After all, you have to give the prince of your dreams a chance to rescue you...

The curtsey

As a princess, you only have to curtsey to people who are more important than you. In other words, hardly anyone! But you do need to curtsey to the king and queen, even if they are your parents...

Your Royal Highnesses...

...only on very formal occasions though, or you'd spend your life bobbing up and down.

I would suggest perfecting your curtsey in private. That way, you won't get caught wobbling in public.

How to make the perfect curtsey...

Hold out your skirt.

Don't forget to smile.

Put your right foot behind your left leg, with just your toes touching the floor.

Gently bend your knees.

You'll earn extra points for teaching your pets how to curtsey.

If you're curtseying to foreign kings and princes, hold out your skirt and raise your right hand to be kissed. Keep your head lowered — this will make you look good and sweet...

...though you could peek through your lashes when curtseying to handsome princes.

Sitting down

You might think you know how to sit down, but there are rules for this too.

Sit with a straight back.

Place your hands neatly in your lap.

?

NEVER slouch.

Keep your knees together.

Keeping a straight back, especially at long banquets, is harder than it looks. The Victorians taught girls to sit up straight by strapping boards to their backs. Perhaps try this on your little brother first, to see if it works.

Only two more hours to go now.

Waving

A princess starts work on her wave at an early age, and once mastered, it need never be changed. Here are some waving styles to choose from:

The "gracious" wave, performed by gently turning the wrist.

The "wiggly fingers" wave: a gentle movement of the fingers keeping your arm still.

The "talk-to-the-hand" wave: raised arm and flat palm.

The "elbow-only" wave – move the forearm in a side-to-side sweep.

The "eager-waver": an energetic shoulder-to-fingertip shake.

Chapter 5
Princess events

Your princess training is nearly over, and you can soon start going to events. But before you whisk yourself off to balls and banquets, there are three words you must remember: MANNERS, MANNERS, MANNERS.

Try being polite to your brothers and sisters. If you can be polite to them, you can be polite to anyone.

Thank you for showing me your tongue. It's a lovely one.

Out and about

When meeting the general public, shake hands and smile sweetly. A princess is polite to everyone, prince or plumber, brave knight or beggar.

Newspaper report of my first royal outing ↘

DAILY ☰ POST

EXCLUSIVE! ☰☰☰

PERFECT PRINCESS

Rosalinda waved and smiled at the crowds at the gala opening, delighting everyone who had come to see her. "She was so polite," said Mrs. Tyler. "Just as a princess should be."

Talking at tea parties

Tea party conversations should be kept light and airy, like the cakes. You should also remember not to raise your voice, and *never* shout, unless it's an emergency.

WE'RE OUT OF CAKE!

Running out of cake, for example, is not an emergency. The three things you can shout are:

1. "FIRE!"

2. "STOP, THIEF!"

3. "RESCUE ME!"
(It helps if you can shout this within the hearing of handsome princes.)

Behaving at banquets

Banquets are very important occasions. You need to be charming and witty and able to keep the conversation flowing. See my top tips below:

1. First, look to see if the queen is talking to the man on her left or right, then copy her.

2. Don't turn your back on a guest – simply turn your head when talking.

Could you pass the salt, please?

3. Remember, you may ONLY speak to the people on either side of you. Never talk to the person opposite you, even if he is the handsome prince of your dreams.

4. Royal menus are in French, so you may want to brush up on your vocab before the banquet.

5. Try not to talk about yourself too much. Instead, begin by asking people questions about themselves.

How NOT to behave

...and at 2:00pm I had my hair done...

6. The best questions are those that get people talking, such as, "Which of your castles do you love most and why?" or "Could you tell me about the time you were turned into a frog?"

Knowing your knives

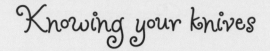

At banquets, it's not just the conversation that you'll need to know how to handle, but the knives and forks too. The basic rule is to start on the outside and work your way in, course by course.

Side plate

Note the different glass sizes

Water glass

Red wine

White wine

Main course fork

Dinner plate

Salad knife

Soup spoon

Salad fork

Dessert fork

Dessert spoon

Main course knife

Bread knife

Starters

At the beginning of a banquet, wait for the queen to be seated, then sit down yourself. Open your napkin and spread it on your knee. If you have an evening purse, place it beneath your napkin.

Be careful not to confuse the napkin with the tablecloth.

Some people prefer to tuck their napkins into their collars. Avoid this technique unless you want to look like a baby wearing a bib.

Soup is often served as a first course. When someone serves you, it will be over your left shoulder, so be prepared.

Tilt the soup bowl away from you
(not too far), then tilt your spoon
and scoop it up.

Don't DRIBBLE
or SLURP and
definitely don't drink
from the bowl.

You can eat bread with your fingers, but make sure you put butter from the butter dish on your side plate, *not* straight onto your bread.

Your Royal Highness is accused of putting butter straight onto her bread.

How awful!

Main courses

The main course will usually be fish or meat.
If you're a vegetarian, make sure the chef knows
before the meal begins.

If you do eat meat, remove it from the bone with your knife and fork, not with your teeth.

Remember you're a princess, not an animal.

If there's a warm bowl of water next to you with some lemon in it, DON'T DRINK IT! It means you'll be served asparagus (the only thing you can eat with your hands apart from bread). The bowl is for rinsing your fingers.

A true tale

Once upon a time, Queen Elizabeth II was at a royal banquet. An important guest thought his finger bowl was a glass of water and drank from it, thirstily. The Queen spotted his mistake and, to save him from embarrassment, she drank from her finger bowl too. Soon, everyone at the table was doing the same.

Desserts and coffee

There is only one word to say about dessert...
YUM!

Just try not to eat too much,
or too fast.

Dessert is usually followed by tea or coffee. Don't drink too much during the banquet though, as it's rude to leave the table, even if you are BURSTING.

After dinner

At the end of the meal, leave your napkin on your chair, then follow the queen out of the room. You can now talk about the other dinner guests, but be careful what you say.

I sat next to Prince Stinkerdink at dinner. He's really smelly.

That's my husband you're talking about!

If the banquet is taking place in your palace, slip down to the kitchens to thank the staff.

Hopefully, the chef will give you some tasty leftovers.

If you are STILL hungry, or just fancy a midnight snack, I can recommend my own recipe below...

Jewelled crown biscuits

Ingredients:

50g (2oz) butter

3 tablespoons golden syrup

175g (6oz) self-raising flour

½ teaspoon ground cinnamon

½ teaspoon bicarbonate
   of soda

1 tablespoon light soft
   brown sugar

2 tablespoons milk

For decorating:
writing icing and sweets

You will also need 2
baking trays.

Makes around 16

Before you start, wipe cooking oil over two baking trays. Heat your oven to 180°C, 350°F, gas mark 4 in step 5.

1 Cut the butter into cubes and put them into a small pan. Add the golden syrup, then gently heat the pan on a low heat.

2 Stir the mixture every now and then, until it has just melted. Then, take the pan off the heat and let it cool for 3 minutes.

3 Sift the flour, cinnamon and bicarbonate of soda into a bowl and stir in the brown sugar. Make a hollow in the middle with a spoon.

4 Carefully pour the butter and syrup mixture into the hollow. Add the milk and stir until it comes together into a ball of dough.

Flatten the dough a little
before you wrap it.

Roll out the dough slowly
but firmly.

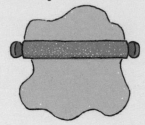

5 Wrap the dough in plastic
foodwrap and put it in
the fridge for 15 minutes.
While the dough is chilling,
turn on your oven.

6 Dust a rolling pin and
a clean work surface with
some flour. Roll out the
dough until it is half as
thick as your little finger.

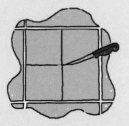

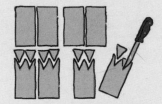

7 Cut off the wobbly edges
of the dough with a sharp
knife, to make a square.
Then, cut the square into
four pieces, like this.

8 Cut each piece in half,
to make a rectangle. Then,
make each rectangle into
a crown by cutting out two
small triangles at the top.

Wear oven gloves.

9 Squeeze the scraps into a ball and roll it out. Cut out more crowns, then put all of the crowns onto the baking trays.

10 Bake the crowns for 8-10 minutes. Carefully lift them out of the oven and leave them on the baking trays for five minutes.

Stick on sweets with dots of icing.

11 Lift the crowns onto a wire rack with a spatula, and let them cool. Then, decorate them with writing icing and sweets for jewels.

Snacks aside, are you ready to sit through a state banquet? Take this test to find out...

Banquet Quiz

1. Your absolute fave food is put in front of you. Do you:

(a) Pick up your plate and lick the platter clean?

(b) Gobble it up as fast as you can? It's not rude. You're just showing that you love it.

(c) Eat it slowly, taking small, dainty mouthfuls?

2. You're sitting next to someone REALLY dull. Do you:

(a) Sigh, cross your arms and stare blankly into space, in the hope he'll get the message?

(b) Talk to the person on your other side instead?

(c) Listen carefully and smile, as if he's the most interesting person in the world?

3. You've been given something revolting to eat.

Do you:

(a) Say "How disgusting!" as loudly as you can?

(b) Pick it up, play with it and turn green?

(c) At least try to eat it, taking very small mouthfuls and frequent sips of water?

4. You have just taken a giant mouthful of food, when the man on your left starts talking to you.

Do you:

(a) Spit it out and chat back?

(b) Talk through your mouthful – it would be rude to keep him waiting?

(c) Smile, nod your head, but wait until you've finished before you start talking?

Mostly As:
Your eating habits are more suited to a barn than a banquet. *Manners, manners, manners!*

Mostly Bs:
I'm afraid you've still got a long way to go before Prince Charming looks at you and sees a true princess.

Mostly Cs:
Your manners are a picture of perfection. Prince Charming will be very impressed.

CONGRATULATIONS!

Your royal wedding

This is the most important event in any princess's life. You have found your prince, which means no more frog-kissing or hunting for peas. Instead, it's time to roll out the red carpet. Here's a step-by-step guide to your wedding day:

1. Choose your tiara

2. Choose your wedding gown (the longer the train the better)

3. Send the invitations

Princess Rosalinda and Prince Charming invite you to their wedding...

4. Choose a cake

5. Get married

6. Pose for photos

7. Wave to the admiring crowd from the balcony

8. Then sit back and relax as you're whisked off to live *HAPPILY EVER AFTER...*

Princess or Peasant Quiz
Which are you?

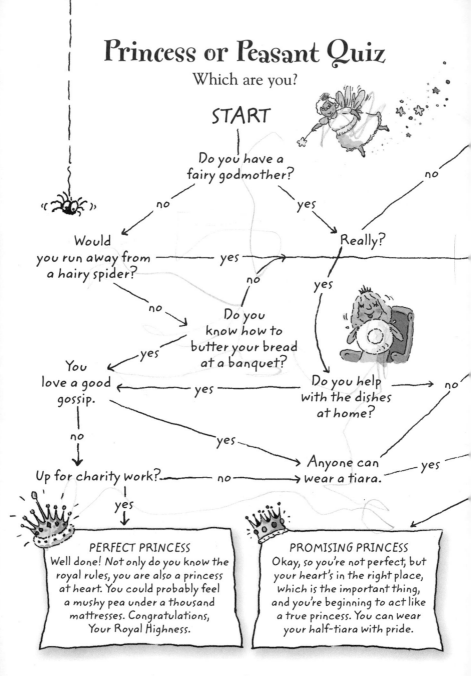

START

Do you have a fairy godmother?

no — Would you run away from a hairy spider? — yes

yes — Really?

no

no

no

yes

Do you know how to butter your bread at a banquet?

yes

yes

You love a good gossip.

yes

Do you help with the dishes at home? — no

no

yes

Up for charity work? — no — Anyone can wear a tiara. — yes

yes

PERFECT PRINCESS
Well done! Not only do you know the royal rules, you are also a princess at heart. You could probably feel a mushy pea under a thousand mattresses. Congratulations, Your Royal Highness.

PROMISING PRINCESS
Okay, so you're not perfect, but your heart's in the right place, which is the important thing, and you're beginning to act like a true princess. You can wear your half-tiara with pride.